With a **moo-moo** here,

and a **moo-moo** there...

Here a **moo**,

there a **moo**,

everywhere
a **moo-moo**.

Old MacDonald had a Farm

Old MacDonald
had a farm, E-I-E-I-O.

And on his farm he had
some cows, E-I-E-I-O.

Old MacDonald
had a farm, E-I-E-I-O.

And on his farm he had some sheep, E-I-E-I-O.

With a **baa-baa** here,

and a **baa-baa** there...

Here a **baa**,

there a **baa**,

everywhere a **baa-baa**.

Old MacDonald
had a farm, E-I-E-I-O.

Old MacDonald had
a farm, E-I-E-I-O.
And on his farm he had
some pigs,

E-I-E-I-O.

With an **oink-oink** here,

and an **oink-oink** there...

Here an **oink**,

there an **oink**,

everywhere an **oink-oink**.

Old MacDonald had a farm, E-I-E-I-O.

Old MacDonald had
a farm, E-I-E-I-O.

And on his farm
he had some hens,

E-I-E-I-O.

With a **cluck-cluck** here,

and a
cluck-cluck
there...

Here a **cluck**,

there
a **cluck**,

everywhere a **cluck-cluck**,

Old MacDonald had a farm, E-I-E-I-O!

Boo!

cock-a-doodle-doo!

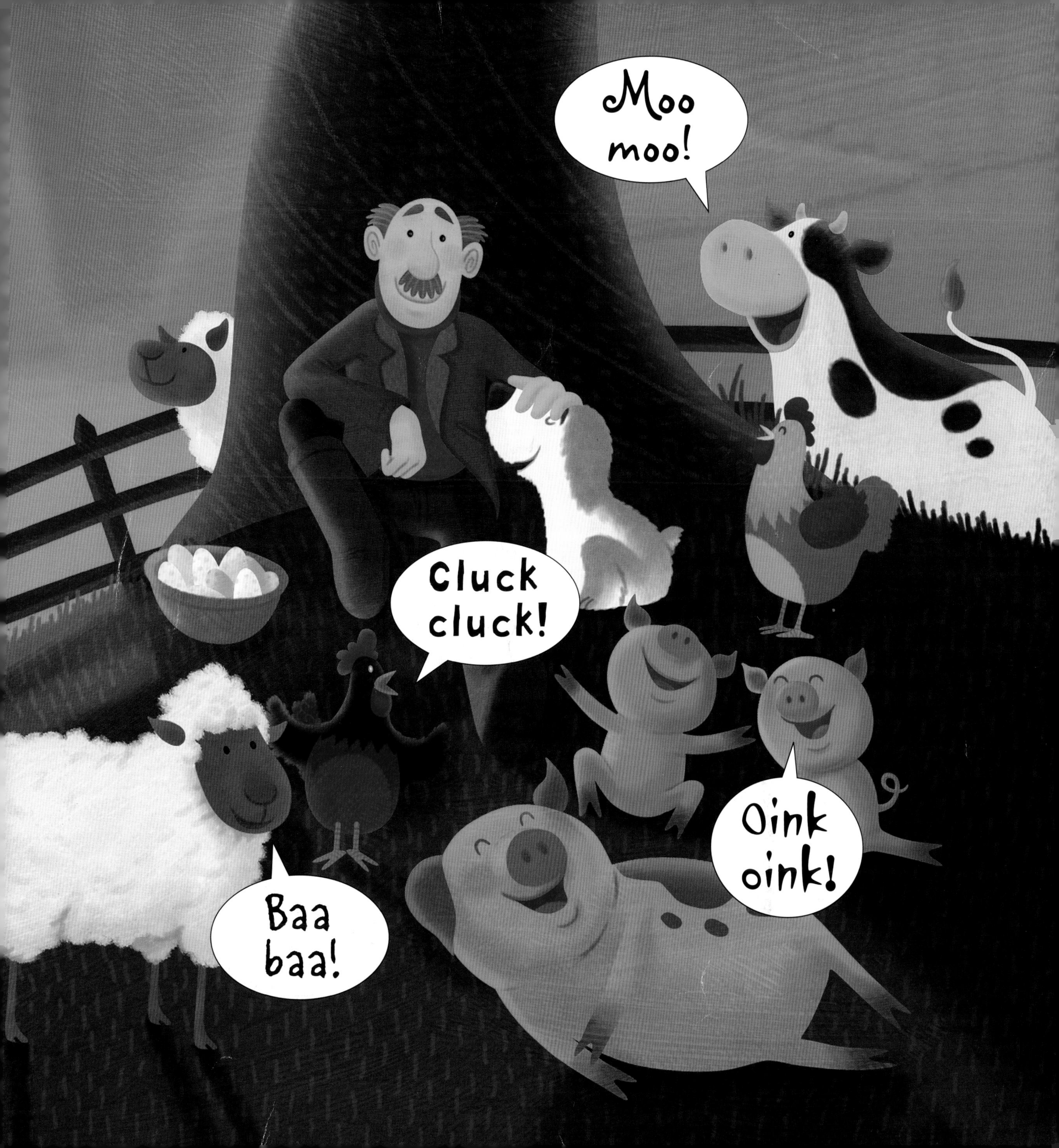
Moo moo!
Cluck cluck!
Oink oink!
Baa baa!

Designed by Caroline Spatz Edited by Lesley Sims
Digital manipulation: Nick Wakeford

This edition first published in 2014 by Usborne Publishing Ltd., Usborne House, 83-85 Saffron Hill, London EC1N 8RT, England.
www.usborne.com Copyright © 2014, 2010 Usborne Publishing Ltd.